For Chloe Sophia Martinez, with love.
In memory of Cheryl White,
the first Black female jockey in the United States.
—M.M.

For my brave and brilliant niece, Nantso—soon you'll
achieve amazing things. Will always be there to support
you. Your favorite auntie.
—S.C.

Text copyright © 2023 by Michelle Meadows

Cover art and interior illustrations copyright © 2023 by Sawyer Cloud

All rights reserved. Published in the United States by Random House Children's Books,
a division of Penguin Random House LLC, New York.

Random House and the colophon and Beginner Books and colophon are registered trademarks
of Penguin Random House LLC. The Cat in the Hat logo ® and © Dr. Seuss Enterprises, L.P.
1957, renewed 1986. All rights reserved.

Visit us on the Web!
rhcbooks.com

Educators and librarians, for a variety of teaching tools, visit us at RHTeachersLibrarians.com

Library of Congress Cataloging-in-Publication Data is available upon request.
ISBN 978-0-593-48316-9 (trade) — ISBN 978-0-593-48317-6 (lib. bdg.) —
ISBN 978-0-593-48318-3 (ebook)

MANUFACTURED IN CHINA
10 9 8 7 6 5 4 3 2 1
First Edition

How to Love a Pony

by Michelle Meadows
illustrated by Sawyer Cloud

BEGINNER BOOKS®
A Division of Random House

Come on down
the dusty lane!
Can you spot
a silky mane?

I am Lily. This is our farm—
full of love and country charm.

In the pasture,

ponies graze.

We show them love

in many ways. . . .

Every autumn,
Pony Day!

Grandpa and I
lead the way.

From the side,

we pet with care.

Braiding manes
and brushing hair.

Apple, carrot,

bale of hay.

Pony rides
and games to play.

Zigzag, zigzag
through the course.
Clip-clop, clip-clop—
clever horse!

Birds fly south.

Leaves disappear.

Goodbye, autumn.

Winter's here.

Every winter,
frost and snow.

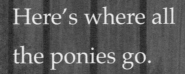

Here's where all
the ponies go.

Planting kisses.

Giving hugs.

Wrapping blankets
known as rugs.

We walk around
the frozen pond
for exercise
and time to bond.

Every spring,
the bluebirds sing.
Baking homemade
treats to bring.

What a greeting!

Love you, too!

A special time
for me and you.

Soapy water
in a pail.

Gentle strokes
from head to tail.

Pick the hooves
for stones and dirt.
I notice when
my pony's hurt.

I introduce a furry friend
while my pony's on the mend.

Feeling better,
on the trail.
Swish, swish, swish—
a braided tail.

Pony picnic
on the ground.
I love my pony
all year round!

Time's gone by—
almost a year.

A foal is born.

New life is here.

Every summer
on the farm . . .
full of love and
country charm.